This book belongs to

....

Peppa Pig™

LADYBIRD BOOKS

UK | USA | Canada | Ireland | Australia | India | New Zealand | South Africa

Ladybird Books is part of the Penguin Random House group of companies
whose addresses can be found at global.penguinrandomhouse.com.

www.penguin.co.uk   www.puffin.co.uk   www.ladybird.co.uk

Penguin
Random House
UK

First published 2020
001

Printed in China

A CIP catalogue record for this book is available from the British Library

ISBN: 978-0-241-44862-5

All correspondence to:
Ladybird Books
Penguin Random House Children's
One Embassy Gardens, 8 Viaduct Gardens, London SW11 7BW

FSC
www.fsc.org

MIX
Paper from
responsible sources
FSC® C018179

Santa's
workshop

Peppa's Night Before Christmas

 **'Twas** the night before Christmas,
And Peppa couldn't sleep.
She crept out of bed . . .
Said, "I'll just take a peep."

Then she went to her window –
Could Santa be heard?
She listened with care . . .
"Oh, it's only a bird!"

Tweet! Tweet!

**She** went back to her bed,
And saw George was awake.
"Look outside!" She pointed.
"Magical snowflakes!"

Wow!

 gazed at the snow.
"San-ta?" he called out.
"Not yet, George," said Peppa,
"But let's look about!"

Then suddenly . . . BANG!
What could that have been?
Had Santa crash-landed?
Or was it a dream?

Then more noises followed, like "Ouch!", "Eek!" and "Yelp!"
"Come quickly!" called Santa.
"Oh, please – I need help!"

 "**My** sleigh lights are broken –
I can't see a thing.
I must give out presents.
It's awful timing!"

 Santa," said Peppa.
"What will light your sleigh?
Might this magical unicorn
Help you find your way?"

"She's perfect!" said Santa.
"Her horn will shine bright.
She'll be back by morning,
Before it gets light."

 sprinkled the magic,
and . . . "Go!" Santa said.
"Now Peppa and George,
You must soon get to bed!"

As they waved him goodbye,
They heard Santa shout:
"Happy Christmas, to you!
Thanks for helping me out!"

"**Oh** George, how amazing!
But our secret, don't tell."
After such an adventure,
They slept very well.

On Christmas Day morning,
All were excited.
The gifts were delivered
And the kids were delighted!

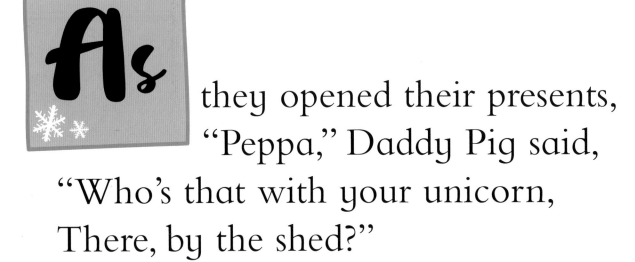 they opened their presents,
"Peppa," Daddy Pig said,
"Who's that with your unicorn,
There, by the shed?"

Peppa winked at George
In the twinkling light.
They'd never forget
Their most magical night!